ROSY COLE:
She Grows and Graduates

Sheila Greenwald

Orchard Books
New York

Orchard Books, 95 Madison Avenue,
New York, NY 10016

Manufactured in the United States of America
Book design by Mina Greenstein
The text of this book is set in 14 point New
Century Schoolbook.
The illustrations are pen-and-ink drawings.
10 9 8 7 6 5 4 3 2 1

Library of Congress Cataloging-in-Publication Data
Greenwald, Sheila.
Rosy Cole : she grows and graduates /
Sheila Greenwald.
    p.   cm.
Summary: While focused entirely on gaining
admittance to the posh Hilyard School next year,
eighth-grader Rosy Cole neglects her friends and her
real talent until she finally makes an important
discovery about herself.
ISBN 0-531-30022-6   ISBN 0-531-33022-2 (lib. bdg.)
[1. Self-acceptance—Fiction.   2. Friendship—Fiction.
3. Schools—Fiction.]   I. Title.
PZ7.G852Rnb   1997
[Fic]—dc21   97-9899

This book is dedicated
with gratitude to the
Fiorello H. La Guardia High School for
Music and Art and the Performing Arts
and to the
public education system of the
City of New York for encouraging
generations of young people to
"grow and graduate."

·1·

Just when I had five good friends and didn't care anymore about being famous or gorgeous. Just when Christy McCurry, who was once my enemy, was my friend. Just when her brother, Donald, whom I liked, liked me. . . .

Just when I got my hair to swing and my body to fill out my uniform. Just when I had an A in English and a B plus in history and was BEST ARTIST in the whole school.

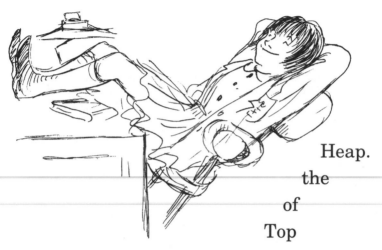

Heap.
the
of
Top

Just when I was finally
I learned that sometimes there's only one place to go from Top of the Heap:

D
O
W
N.

My name is Rosy Cole. I attend Miss Read's School. Miss Read's is a small private school on the Upper East Side of Manhattan. Once Miss Read's went from kindergarten right through high school. Now it stops at the eighth grade.

"We are Top of the Heap," I said to my friends Hermione Wong and Christy McCurry on the first day of eighth grade.

"Top of the Heap," Hermione said, agreeing with me for once. We laughed and shook hands and adjusted our knapsacks and headed off to school.

Our teacher, Mrs. Oliphant, greeted us with a big smile. "Good morning, girls," she said as soon as we were seated.

"Good morning, Mrs. Oliphant," we said, smiling back.

"How exciting!" she exclaimed. "You are the senior class at Miss Read's. This term you will embark on the adventure of selecting the school where your individual talents can flourish next year." She turned to the blackboard and began to write as she talked.

"Soon you will schedule appointments for the visits and tours, interviews and tests that will help you to determine which school is best for you." She rubbed her hands together. "The next months will be full of ups and downs and highs and lows, but there is one thing for sure. By graduation day every one of you will have chosen your new school. Every one of you will have grown and changed."

By now Mrs. Oliphant was the only person in the room who was still smiling. Who wanted to choose a new school? Who wanted to grow and change?

"I know you've all been thinking about this," Mrs. Oliphant went on.

WRONG.

"I know you've all been considering the schools you wish to apply to."

WRONG.

"I know you've all been concerned about the ERB and the SA tests," she continued. "That's the Educational Records Board and Stanford Achievement."

To me it sounded more like the Everything Really Bad and Scary Also.

1. Visits
2. Tours
3. Interviews
4. Tests

"So I want to reassure you that whatever your scores — high, low, or in between — you will find the right place for your very own level."

The right place for our very own level? I looked around at my friends. Debbie had straight A's. Linda had C's. Keisha, Hermione, and I were in the middle with A's in subjects we liked and B's and C's in those we didn't.

What was Mrs. Oliphant smiling about? We were going to be separated by our grades. We weren't just US anymore, but US with numbers attached, like a price tag or a rating — first, second, or third.

At recess, Natalie Pringle announced, "I'm all set. My whole family has gone to Fogley. My aunt Dinah is on the board, and my mother registered me at birth."

"So did mine," Jenny Gilchrist squealed. "My aunt Trish is on the board, too."

They hugged each other and jumped up and down with joy. "We'll both be going to Fogley."

Registered at *birth?*

Aunts on the board?

Mrs. Oliphant hadn't written that on the blackboard.

"When I was born, my mother just registered me at City Hall along with everyone else," Debbie tried to joke. "She must have guessed you can't get into Fogley unless you know somebody."

Natalie and Jenny grinned. *They* both knew somebody.

"My sisters went to Paxton," I said. "That's where I know someone."

"Big deal," Natalie said, looking at Jenny. "Paxton takes anybody from Read."

"You're a fine one to talk," Debbie said. "You just told us Fogley takes anyone with a relative on the board. It isn't like Hilyard, where you need to have a brain."

That stopped Natalie cold. "A brain?"

"B-R-A-I-N," Debbie spelled out.

"I don't think any of us could get into Hilyard." Jenny shook her head. "It's the tops. They've got a waiting list a mile long. All the parents are in *People* magazine. Three hours of homework a night. Everybody competing for the best grades to get into the best colleges."

Best colleges, interviews, tests, waiting lists a mile long. Top of the Heap was

suddenly turning into

1. VISITS
2. TOURS
3. INTERVIEWS
4. TESTS

the pits.

Since it was the first day of school, we were dismissed before lunch. Debbie and Linda and Christy and Keisha and Hermione and I headed over to Vinnie's for a pizza.

We found our usual table and reserved it with our jackets. Then we got slices and sodas and sat down. But nobody ate.

"I'm going to take the test for CitiArt," Hermione said slowly. "It's public and free, and if I get accepted for music, I'll have special classes and time to study the cello."

"I'll try for CitiTech," Debbie decided.

"It's public and free and gives advanced courses in math and science."

"Oh no," Linda wailed. "Next fall we'll all be in different schools." She covered her face with her hands. "This is the first day of the last good year of our lives." From behind her hands we heard a sob.

"Wait a minute," Christy said brightly. "I have an idea. Why not apply to the same school? One we know we can all get into."

Hermione and Debbie frowned, but Linda came out from behind her hands, smiling.

Keisha raised her root beer. "Here's to next year at Paxton," she said. We all toasted one another, as if we were making a promise and had just solved a big problem for good.

But I had a feeling we hadn't solved a thing, and for me the problem was just beginning.

CitiArt was for music and art. CitiTech was for math and science. Hilyard was tops. You needed a B-R-A-I-N. Did I have a brain? Could I be tops? Did I want to find out?

·2·

Walking home from Vinnie's, Christy said, "I'm glad we all decided not to apply to Hilyard. Hillys are snobs."

Trust Christy to have the inside scoop. Until then I had no idea that Hilyard girls were "Hillys," and snobs on top of it.

"How do you know?" Hermione asked.

"Donald's new girlfriend, Beatrice Best, is a Hilly."

DONALD'S NEW GIRLFRIEND!

"What's the matter with you, Rosy?" Hermione took my arm. "You look like you were run over by a truck."

How could she even ask? Didn't she remember about Donald and *me*?

For years, every time I looked at Christy's older brother, Donald, I got as fizzy as soda water. For years he always seemed to be thinking about something so important, he never looked back. Then last spring I bumped into him at the museum, where I was trying to learn from works of art how to make myself as beautiful as his sisters, Christy and Dawn.

"You don't need to paint yourself like a billboard the way Christy and Dawn do to be pretty," Donald said. It was Donald who showed me my beauty type in one of the paintings,

and helped me achieve the

look of the portrait with lots of practice
and a little home perm.

Donald told me I was more fun to be
with than any other girl. Later, when all
I was doing was gazing in the mirror, he
let me know he was disappointed and val-
ued my friendship over my looks.

Donald used to call me almost every

day to talk about art or music or poetry. But since last month, when he'd started at CitiArt, he phoned me only once — to tell me he found he wanted to become a great painter like Picasso.

Now I wondered, had he also found a girl who was more fun to be with than me?

"Since when does Donald have this new girlfriend?" Hermione wanted to know.

"Since a week ago when he met her at the Hilyard Harvest Dance. Her name is Beatrice Best. For seven days she has been camped at our house. She calls Donald 'Donadeo' and 'Chéri.' She has an IQ of a zillion, and people worship at her PSAT scores."

Hermione gave my arm a squeeze. "We better check her out," she said softly.

Christy lives in the same building as me and Hermione, so all we had to do was step off the elevator at her floor. For me it was as if I was about to step into a jungle full of wild beasts.

As Christy put her key in the latch, we heard someone laughing inside the apartment. It was the wild beast, all right.

"I forgot to mention, he's painting her portrait for his class in oils," Christy whispered.

"So she's just homework." Hermione gave me a comforting wink.

Donald's "homework" was sitting on a stool in the middle of his room with a bottle of lime seltzer in her hand. *"Bonjour, bonjour, les enfants."* She waved to us through the half-open door.

Christy barged right in. "I'd like you to meet my friends Rose and Hermione."

Donald was at his easel, painting *Girl with Seltzer*.

Beatrice Best rushed up to me. "Donald has told me all about you, Rose." She grabbed my chin in her hand and turned my face this way and that. "And he was sooo right. You *could* be a Pre-Raphaelite maiden." She called over to Donald, "Her complexion is that pale and her eyes that mournful." Beatrice squinted at me again, looking for more signs of how miserable I was. "She is a walking portrait

by Dante Gabriel Rossetti."

"Rosy is our class artist," Hermione boasted. "She fills all her notebooks with great doodles. Her cartoons and comics are so good you can't tell them from the ones in the newspapers."

"Rosy has talent." Donald nodded, turning his green eyes on my face, the way he had in the museum when he made me promise to follow his beauty advice. "But she has to develop a style of her own by using her own eyes to see that art is all around her. Right now, her work is too derivative."

"Derivative?" Christy rolled her eyes and groaned, indicating the word was not in her vocabulary.

"It means she copies, dear," Beatrice explained with an eye roll of her own, indicating she thought Christy was a moron. "A good teacher could change that."

"Exactly right," Donald agreed. "Most gifted young artists copy. But at CitiArt we learn to appreciate and emulate the masters of great art, not cartoons. Rosy should take the test for CitiArt, even though it isn't easy."

"But we've all agreed to go to Paxton," Christy told her brother.

"Paxton!" Beatrice scoffed. "They don't have a decent art department."

"What about Hilyard?" I finally got a word in.

"Hilyard?" Beatrice gasped as if I'd said "law school." "It's so academically challenging, I wouldn't recommend it to anyone who didn't have a natural desire to study, study, study."

At that moment I had a natural desire to shove my Hilyard acceptance letter in Beatrice Best's smiling, snooty face that Donald was painting in oils.

I could tell she didn't think I was smart enough for Hilyard and Donald didn't think I was talented enough for CitiArt. Then and there I wanted more than anything to prove that they were both wrong.

"Buzz me when the Hilly leaves," I whispered to Christy as I headed out the door.

I had a lot to do, and there wasn't a moment to lose.

·3·

At home, my sisters, Anitra and Pippa, were getting ready to go back to their colleges upstate the next day. Anitra was cutting holes in her new blue jeans, and Pippa was ironing patches over the holes she'd made just last year.

Donald was right. Art was all around me. If I really looked, I would develop a style of my own.

Drawing from life *was* different from copying. Donald was right again. I had to use my eyes more. I had to totally concentrate.

To be honest, though I always loved to doodle, I never thought about it much. Then last year, everybody started noticing my pictures and asking me to draw for them. "Oh, Rosy, can you draw me in my favorite comic strip, or do the Little Mermaid or Belle from *Beauty and the Beast* or Pocahontas, just like in the movies?" Soon I was called "class artist" and "best artist in the school."

Drawing made me popular. It made me important. But class artist? How could anything be important that was that easy? Important things are *hard*. Drawing for me was just fun.

I was so deep in my portrait of Anitra and Pippa it was as if the clock had stopped.

"I have a million things to do," Pippa complained. "I can't stand at this ironing board forever."

"We haven't even packed yet," Anitra whined.

GIRL CUTTING NEW HOLES AND GIRL IRONING PATCHES OVER OLD HOLES

I guess I was the only one who thought the clock had stopped. But when I showed my sisters the portrait, they were impressed.

"It's your best yet," Pippa cried. Anitra agreed.

In fact, I was so amazed at my work, I wondered if CitiArt would take me without a test. I could hardly wait to show Donald.

It was practically dark when Christy

finally buzzed me on the house phone. "The Hilly's gone," she whispered.

I grabbed my sketch pad and ran out the door and down the staircase. Too impatient to wait for an elevator.

When I burst into Donald's room he was putting away his brushes and paints.

"I've taken your advice," I panted. "Art is all around me, and I've drawn from life. Just *look!*"

He placed my work beside his own on the easel and stood back a few paces. "Better," he finally decided, with a serious smile. "But you're still not using your own eyes enough."

"I am the best artist in my whole school," I informed him. My voice was all wobbly.

"Then you need a better school," Donald advised, as if it were obvious. "You need CitiArt."

I took a deep breath. "If CitiArt is a place where people hurt each other's feelings, I'll skip it."

Donald blinked in surprise. "CitiArt is a place where you learn to take criticism, Rosy. It's a place where you learn how to draw by using your own eyes, not by imitating the work of others."

"You should know about imitating others." My voice had gone from wobbling to cracking, I was that upset.

Donald looked puzzled, as if he didn't even know how he'd insulted me. "What do you mean?"

I was too choked up with emotion to speak, so I took the charcoal stick off his easel and signed his portrait of *Girl with Seltzer*.

Donald's face turned red and then pale. I knew I'd scored a major hit. "Maybe you're right," he said, nodding, "but at least I'm imitating *good* art."

"What do you mean?" I asked.

He took the charcoal out of my hand and wrote on my drawing.

I snatched my work off the easel and ran for the door before he could see the wet stuff that was all over my cheeks and think I was crying.

Out in the hall, I looked at the portrait of my sisters, and I didn't like it anymore, either.

I was sure Donald would never have talked to Beatrice Best the way he did to me. She wasn't just "class artist" with a trick for cartooning. She was TOPS. A Hilly with a BRAIN.

Back at my apartment, Anitra and Pippa were setting the table for dinner. My parents were cooking.

"Why did you choose Paxton?" I asked my sisters.

"Because they took us," Anitra said.

"What about Hilyard?"

"I couldn't finish the math part of that test if my life depended on it," Pippa said, laughing. "And Daddy isn't rich or famous."

"What does rich and famous have to do with it?"

"The right numbers in your parents' bank account will correct the wrong ones on the math exam," Anitra explained.

"If your essay is boring, but your mother's novel is a best-seller, you don't have to worry about getting into Hilyard," Pippa added.

"Or anyplace else," Anitra agreed. "Even so, Hilyard is the toughest school in town no matter how you get in. Don't set your heart on Hilyard. It may not be right for you."

"With the highest tuition in the city, it's not right for *me*," Dad chimed in.

My mother closed her eyes and smiled. "If I had a daughter at Hilyard, my friends would turn green with envy."

"And your family would turn blue from bank loans," Dad mumbled.

My mother opened her eyes. "What about Paxton?" she said in her down-to-earth voice.

"Anybody from Read can go to Paxton."
I was at the end of my rope. "I am not
anybody from Read. I am *somebody* from
Read."

They all stared at me as if they didn't
know *who* I was.

In a way I couldn't blame them. Only
that morning I was Top of the Heap. Now
I could see that from Top of the Heap I
still had mountains to climb and no one
to help.

·4·

Monday morning, it came to me! There *was* someone who could help. I counted the minutes all day till I could see her.

Mrs. BOBER
GUIDANCE
COUNSELOR

"Rosy Cole." Mrs. Bober, the guidance counselor of our school, greeted me with a surprised smile. "You are the very first person in your class to see me."

"That's because I want to go to Hilyard, and I know there is a lot to do."

Mrs. Bober stopped smiling. "Oh, Rosy, Hilyard has a waiting list around the block. I've never been able to get a Read student accepted."

"Then I could be the first."

"Of course, they give preference to children of alumni and siblings," Mrs. Bober said hopefully. "Have you any family members who are graduates?"

"Not yet."

"Then it's a good thing you're making an early start." She opened a large directory of schools that was on her desk and turned to the Hilyard page. " 'Hilyard requires excellent grades,' " she began to read. " 'High test scores. Community service, athletic skill, and a well-rounded personality.' "

I wrote all this down in my new Project Hilyard notebook.

" 'Pick up a catalog and make out an application as soon as possible.' "

She flipped through the directory. "There are so many other good schools here, Rosy. Schools where you could be happy and I could be of real help to you in getting in."

"You *have* been of real help," I said, standing up to go.

"How?" She looked puzzled.

"You've told me what I must do." I held up my notebook to show her and headed for the door. I hadn't a moment to lose.

It was three o'clock. I needed to hurry in order to slip out of school before my friends. That way I could stop off at Hilyard on my way home and pick up the application and the catalog.

Hilyard is in a building I pass every day walking to Read. To me it looked just like my school or Paxton or Fogley. The girls I saw going in and out looked just like Paxton and Fogley girls, too. But from the moment I stepped through the door,

I knew there was something about them that made them special.

Was it the walk? The smile? The hair? A certain something that was hard to describe? Whatever, there was no doubt about it. They had HILYARD written all over them, and since having HILYARD written all over you tells the world you are TOPS, I couldn't wait for the day when I would have HILYARD written all over me, too.

Clutching my catalog and application, I ran all the way home. I didn't want to lose a minute.

I had spread the application out on my desk and was lifting my pen to write when Mike, the doorman, buzzed from the downstairs lobby. "Get out the Kleenex," he said. "It's Linda Dildine on her way up."

I hid my application under the blotter and went to answer the door.

Linda stood on the welcome mat. "My parents are making me break my promise to you and all my friends," she blubbered. "They say I have to apply to Hilyard."

"That's not so terrible." I took Linda by the hand and led her into the kitchen for a glass of water. "Maybe we'll all apply to Hilyard, too."

"But I'll never get in. I don't have the grades. I'm bad at those tests. I'm bad at interviews. I'll fail."

"Don't say that. You shouldn't put your-self down," I advised. "Try to think about your gifts."

Linda stopped crying and leaned over the table, her eyes shining with antici-pation. "What are my gifts, Rosy?" she asked. "I always thought I was a hopeless case."

Actually, she had a point. Linda's grades are bad to awful. She plays the piano in a way that makes you want to run out of the room. Every other minute she bursts into tears.

"You have this great gift," I said slowly, watching the tears drying on her cheeks and thinking hard, "for . . . for feelings."

"Oh, Rosy." She burst out crying again. "I knew you would cheer me up." She looked at the kitchen clock. "I wish I didn't have to go home. I wish I could stay here and we could trade places, and I could be you." She stood up. At least she wasn't crying anymore.

As we walked to the door, I put my arm around her shoulders. I felt so sorry for her.

"I mean, it doesn't make sense, just because all my aunts and cousins went to Hilyard and Mummy went to Hilyard and is on the board of directors and a big contributor to the Alumni Fund and is best friends with the admissions director, is that a reason for me to go there?" As she spoke, she stood in front of the elevator, waving good-bye.

I waved back, suddenly feeling a lot less sorry for Linda.

When I sat back down to fill out page
two of the Hilyard application, I actually
wished we could trade places.

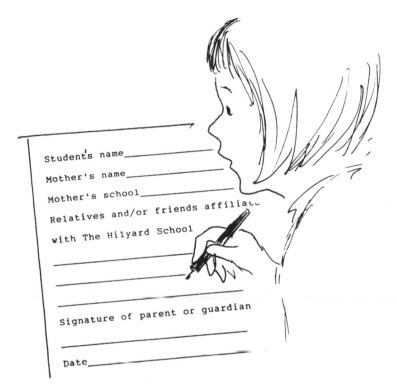

Student's name_____
Mother's name_____
Mother's school_____
Relatives and/or friends affiliated
with The Hilyard School
_____
_____
_____
Signature of parent or guardian
_____
_____
Date_____

If I were Linda, page two of my application would look a lot better than if I were
Rosy Cole.

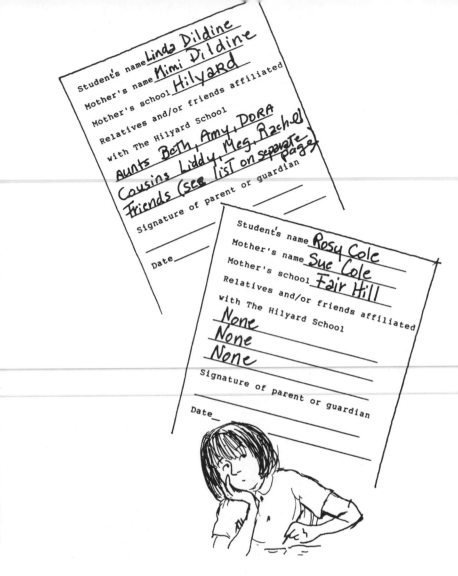

Student's name Linda Dildine
Mother's name Mimi Dildine
Mother's school Hilyard
Relatives and/or friends affiliated
with The Hilyard School
Aunts Beth, Amy, Dora
Cousins Liddy, Meg, Rachel
Friends (see list on separate page)

Signature of parent or guardian
_____

Date_____ _____

Student's name Rosy Cole
Mother's name Sue Cole
Mother's school Fair Hill
Relatives and/or friends affiliated
with The Hilyard School
None
None
None

Signature of parent or guardian
_____

Date_ _____

Halfway through filling out the form, I began to wonder. If only my mother had grown up in the city instead of Fair Hill, she probably would have gone to Hilyard. If she had gone to Hilyard, so would Anitra and Pippa. After I fixed the page to show what would have happened if things had been different, it looked better . . . except at the bottom, where I saw a problem.

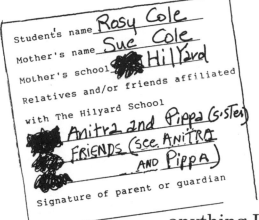

Student's name _Rosy Cole_

Mother's name _Sue Cole_

Mother's school ~~███~~ _Hilyard_

Relatives and/or friends affiliated with The Hilyard School

Anitra and Pippa (sisTers) FRIENDS (see ANiTRA AND PippA)

Signature of parent or guardian

"I never sign anything I haven't read," my mother said, scanning the application before she took up a pen, filled in the line, and handed back the page.

Signature of parent or guardian

The Tooth Fairy

Date _April Fools'_

"When you've written the truth," she said, "I'll sign the truth."

While I waited to pick up a fresh application the next day, I got busy studying the catalog and preparing my room. I needed calendars and lists to help me in my new life plan.

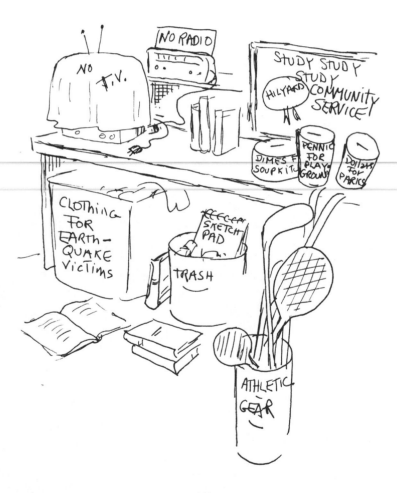

By dinnertime I had already checked off two items on my list. Next was the Hilyard Open House. I already knew one person I would see there. I could hardly wait to find out who else would turn up.

·5·

Guess who else turned up.

"I'm just here for Linda's sake," Christy whispered through a mouth full of assorted cookies.

Keisha agreed. "For Linda's sake. Poor Linda."

"Poor Linda." We nodded, watching her accept a cookie from the admissions director.

We all gave "poor Linda" the thumbs-up sign — as if she needed it.

When we were seated in the auditorium, the admissions director, Dr. McMasters, welcomed us with a slide presentation. "Because one picture is worth a thousand words," she explained, "I must rely on my visual aids."

The slides showed that Hilyard girls were not only tops in academics, but also community service–minded, athletic, generous, ingenious, self-sufficient, and dedicated.

After the presentation, a student guide named Susan took us on a tour of the school. She showed us the classrooms and the gym, library, science labs, and art room.

The art room was large and light. One look at the student work and I knew I would be the best artist at Hilyard. I drew better in third grade. "Nice room," I commented.

"I never get to use it," Susan sighed. "What with all the homework, I have no time for art. Everybody here is so smart. If you don't study more than they do, you won't be as smart or smarter." She stopped to catch her breath.

I wrote all this down. "Anything else?" I asked.

"If you're going to be a Hilly, you'd better be strong and confident, poised and prepared," Susan advised. "But most of all, Hillys have to know how to make

every single second count every single day."
I underlined her words.

I decided to follow Susan's advice, even though it meant giving up even more than I had intended.

A few days later, Hermione noticed that she was one òf the things I had given up.

"Why don't you wait to walk to school anymore?" she complained. "Why do you go home by yourself? Why do you stay in study hall instead of eating lunch? Why didn't you come for a slice with us at Vinnie's on Friday? I never even see you in the building elevator."

"I review math on the walk to school and social studies going home. I gave up lunch to drill for quizzes and Vinnie's for my community service. Elevator rides are for spelling lists."

Hermione shook her head in disbelief. "You're missing out," she said.

She was right.

I almost missed seeing Donald in the elevator until he spoke.

"I apologize for the way I reacted when you criticized my art, Rosy," he began. "I would be interested to know what you think of my latest painting."

"I don't have time for art just now," I murmured.

Another thing I didn't have time for was the fizzy feeling Donald always gave me, but there wasn't anything I could do about it, so I followed him off the elevator at his floor.

In the middle of Donald's room on the easel was the new work. "You were right about *Beatrice I*," he admitted. "I *was* imitating Picasso. But this time I tried to find my own style. How do you like *Beatrice II*?"

"I don't care if she's Beatrice one or fifty," I said. "I told you I don't have time for art right now."

"No time for art?" Donald was amazed. "How can you have no time for the person you really are?"

"Only till December," I assured him. "By then my plan to get accepted to Hilyard should begin to pay off."

"Hilyard?" Donald hooted. "You don't belong there, Rosy! You are an artist whom I respect for her very fine eye."

"I'd rather be a Hilly whom you respect for her very fine brain." I headed for the door.

"You're going against your nature," Donald warned sadly as I waved good-bye.

Maybe I was going against my nature, but I was ahead of my schedule. By the middle of October, Mrs. Oliphant called me to her desk. "Your work has improved remarkably," she congratulated me. "Every single paper is an A or an A plus." She paused and frowned. "But Rosy, I'm worried. You never go to the art room. There are no more doodles in the margins of your notebooks. You look so pale and thin."

Mrs. Oliphant was right. In the mirror, I could see I was skinny from giving up lunch and pale from giving up after-school dates. Also, my nails were bitten.

It was hard not to draw.

By the last week in November I was tied with Debbie for tops in the class. My mother read my report card and gasped. "You've gained ten grade points and lost eight pounds. Not to mention all your friends."

"This has gone far enough," Dad said. "Time to relax."

"How about that pajama party you always wanted, the night before Thanksgiving vacation?" My mother clapped her hands with delight at the thought of it.

"Not now . . . ," I began, looking at my schedule. "I've only got a few weeks till the test."

"We'll order out a three-foot hero," she said, "and rent a video, anything you like."

"All right," I agreed. I had a video in mind. My parents were right; a party was a good idea.

I spent a whole afternoon preparing.

Everyone came early.

"Oh, Rosy, it's like old times," Hermione gushed. "Nobody's been to your place for months. I can't wait to see the surprise video."

Debbie craned her neck to get a look at the dining-room table. "A three-foot hero!" she exclaimed. "You always have the best food."

"But the real treat comes later," I promised.

"Brownies?" Debbie licked her lips.

Halfway through the three-foot hero, I

handed out personalized study kits.

"Study kits?" Keisha groaned. "You promised a video."

"There is a video," I said, holding it up as proof. *"Six Steps to Super Scores.* Finish your

food up fast. We have a full program of review to get through tonight."

Linda pushed her kit aside. "They say you can't prepare for those tests."

"I'll prove they're wrong," I assured her.

"I think I'm coming down with something." Christy began to wrap up what was left of her hero.

"Me, too," Keisha said.

"It's Thanksgiving vacation," Hermione hollered at me as if I were deaf. "There's a special on tonight. I like to watch them blow up the balloons for tomorrow's parade."

"Don't go," I pleaded. "We could watch the show as a treat if we finish the work on time."

"Okay, Rosy." Keisha shook her head in a resigned way. "It's your party."

Christy slowly unwrapped her hero and took a bite.

First we watched the video. Then I had them form a circle on the floor so we could go round-robin with questions from sample exams while the kitchen timer ticked. "It's like *Beat the Clock*," I said, laughing, after the third round. "See how much fun it is to prepare for tests?"

"When can we stop having this fun?" Christy asked. "The TV special is half over."

"Soon we'll break for a bedtime snack," I promised. "And then it's sweet dreams."

But Hermione and Debbie were up half the night with nightmares. Christy broke out in hives. Keisha and Linda had upset stomachs.

In the morning, my friends came into the kitchen as I was mixing up a batter for pancakes.

"That was some pajama party," Christy said with a yawn. "But thanks anyway."

"Two weeks from now, when we take the test, is when you'll really thank me," I told her. "But we still haven't done the flash cards."

"Flash cards?" Debbie blinked.

Everybody headed for the door, waving good-bye. Nobody wanted pancakes.

On the morning of the exam, my mother tried to calm me down. "Just think of the test as practice for the stresses of adult life," she said.

When I got to the Standardized Testing Office, I was amazed to see who else was waiting to "practice for the stresses of adult life."

"Poor things," Keisha whispered.

I disagreed. "I'm sorry my mother didn't start testing me as a baby. That way I would have been even better prepared."

"Prepared?" Linda let out a wail. "I forgot my number-two pencil."

It was a good thing I had an extra. Debbie and Keisha and Hermione offered her tissues and cough drops, and we went into the testing room.

I lined up my bubble sheet with my question sheet and got to work, filling in

the little circles as fast as I could.

All my work really paid off. I was finished a whole seven minutes before poor Linda.

She sat chewing the end of her pencil,
rubbing her red nose and
sighing until the bell
rang and the woman
said,
"Time!"

That was when I
saw that I had
not

really lined up
my bubble sheet
with my question sheet.

All the way home, it wasn't Linda who was crying. "Cheer up," she told me. "At least your parents aren't dying for you to get into Hilyard. At least no one will be brokenhearted when you're turned down."

Guess again.

My friends tried to comfort me. "Who cares about that test anyway?" Hermione laughed. "As long as I pass the CitiArt exam for music and show I have a B-plus average from Read, I'm in."

"If I make CitiTech, that's where I'll

go," Debbie said. "Otherwise Paxton. Who needs Hilyard and scores through the roof?"

I did, that's who. Debbie was a fine one to talk. She didn't need scores through the roof. She already had them.

"Remember that promise we made to stick together?" Linda sighed. "Let's just promise to stay friends, no matter where we end up."

This time when we promised, nobody crossed her fingers.

At home I collapsed on my bed. Tacked to the wall facing me was my list.

I still had the interview ahead of me. Only twenty minutes to turn everything around. How could I do it? I buried my face in the pillow, closed my eyes, and saw shapes and fantastic colors that reminded me of a picture and how *"One picture is worth a thousand words."* It was time for visual aids.

·6·

The morning of the interview, my mother offered to come along and help carry my stuff.

"I can handle it," I said, showing her.

She hugged me and kissed me at the door. "You don't need all of this, Rosy," she said. "Just be your own sweet self."

I didn't tell her that sweetness was not listed in the Hilyard catalog as necessary for admission.

In her office Dr. McMasters sat behind a large desk. "Come in, Rosy," she greeted me, pointing to a chair. "Sit right down and tell me something about yourself."

"To follow the advice you gave us at the open house, I need to stand," I said.

"Excuse me?" She seemed puzzled.

ONE PICTURE IS WORTH A THOUSAND WORDS. RELY ON VISUAL AIDS.

R. COLES ACADEMIC PROGRESS

So I had to remind her.

"I can see by your record that you have done well at school." Dr. McMasters was going through a folder on her desk. "But your score on the ERB is very low."

"Oh, that score doesn't mean anything," I explained. "I just mismatched the bubble sheet to the question sheet."

"Too bad," she sighed, still not looking at my exhibit. "Here at Hilyard we feel that following instructions on an exam is as much a part of the test as the questions themselves."

I couldn't believe she meant what she had said. It sounded so *dumb!*

"But"—she smiled brightly as if she had some wonderful news—"I see you are interested in art."

"Not anymore," I assured her. "I haven't time for art. It got in the way of my academic work."

"But the arts are very important to us at Hilyard. In fact, we have a student who is a violin prodigy. Last year, she showed her generosity, dedication, and ingenuity by giving the Allie Lun Benefit Concert to raise scholarship tuition for the school." Dr. McMasters stood up from her desk, still smiling, and I saw that what she was showing *me* was the door.

Outside her office on a long bench were Linda and her mother, waiting to go in.

"Oh, Rosy." Linda grabbed my hand. "Can you imagine my bad luck? Mummy and McMasters were in the *same* class."

I was tired of imagining Linda's bad luck. I had enough of my own. I had blown the ERB. I had blown the interview. What was left? How could I show my self-reliance, ingenuity, originality, dedication, and generosity?

On my way home from Hilyard, I stopped into Vinnie's for a slice and a soda. It felt like months since I had been there. In fact, it had been. I took a small round table near the window and sat wondering how everything had gone wrong and what I could do to show Hilyard I could be a perfect Hilly. I took out my pencil and notebook to jot down ideas, but instead I drew the chair and the table and Vinnie behind the counter and started to feel a little better. Drawing always calms me down.

"Nice pictures," Vinnie called. "You got a real talent for art."

A real talent for art? Even Dr. McMasters approved of art and gifted students like Allie Lun, the violin-playing prodigy.

Suddenly I saw that the answer to my problem was staring me in the face. In

my pocket was all the allowance I had been too busy studying to spend.

Now I could use it to buy what I needed in order to show Hilyard I was as dedicated, generous, and ingenious as ten Allie Luns.

•7•

I needed posters for the lobby.

Not to mention the work of the prodigy.

My friends and family helped me out. I did Hermione and her cello. Linda at the piano. Debbie and Keisha on the couch. A bowl of fruit with my sisters and a Christmas cactus plant with Mom and Dad.

"How come all your portraits are in black and white, front face and above the neck?" Hermione asked.

"Because I like them that way," I said. She didn't have to know I liked them that way because I couldn't do color or hands or feet or profiles.

I called Donald to ask if he would pose.

"Not a chance," he snapped.

"But I'm taking your advice," I said. "I'm drawing from life."

"I never told you to draw from life for *Hilyard*," he said, and hung up on me.

"All I need now is gallery space," I told my mother.

"I think she's talking about our living room," Dad said. "You can have it for one day." He held up one finger, meaning that the day after, the room had better be a living room again.

I placed my pictures inside the frames that were already hanging on the wall, covering my parents' paintings. Then I put green stickers on the corners telling the price. Red stickers would go on when a picture was sold. Anitra and Pippa helped me pull the furniture away from the walls. Dad put a vase filled with flowers on top of the piano.

"All you need now are refreshments," my mother said. "I'll take care of that for you, Rosy. It's not every day we have an art show opening in our living room. Who knows, you may just draw a real crowd."

As it turned out, I did.

Hermione came with Mrs. Wong. Debbie and Keisha brought Debbie's father. Christy brought her sister, Dawn. There

were five people from the building whom I didn't even know, and our neighbor Mrs. Rapposo came. "This is so much better than when you played the violin." She made a sound like a yowling cat and covered her ears with her hands. But when Linda Dildine walked in with her mother and Dr. McMasters, I knew my idea had paid off. Linda had told her mother. Her mother had asked McMasters.

"What an ingenious young person you are, Rosy," Dr. McMasters complimented me as she helped herself to a cookie. After she suggested that Mrs. Dildine purchase my portrait of Linda, she gave me a wink, as if we were already on the same team.

After one hour, everybody was leaving. There were red stickers on all but two pictures, and my cash box was full.

Just when I thought nothing could get better, Donald stepped through the door.

Donald made a complete circle of the room. He spent at least a minute in front of each of my drawings.

"There are still two that aren't sold," I said. "Is there something you want to buy?"

Donald nodded. "Your leftover stickers. I could use them in a collage."

"You can have the stickers for free." I laughed, trying to make it a joke and pretend I wasn't hurt he didn't love my work.

Donald took the sheets of stickers and put them in his pocket. "Thanks a million, Rosy," he said. "I came to your show, and now it's time for you to come to mine."

"Why not?" Since I had a feeling Hilyard was a sure thing, along with Donald's respect for my Brain, the least I could do was show respect for his art.

The show Donald took me to was the Semiannual CitiArt Exhibit.

Inside CitiArt there were rooms full of easels and rooms full of drawing boards. There were rooms with pianos for the music students and an auditorium set up for an orchestra to perform.

The exhibition gallery was hung with student work. In the middle of the wall, I spotted a familiar face.

"Why is Beatrice Best on loan?" I wondered. "Has someone taken her away from you?"

"On loan means she had to lend me the painting, because I sold it to her. She wanted to give it to her parents for an anniversary gift. She was my first commission."

"Commission? I thought she was your new girlfriend."

"New girlfriend?" Donald burst out laughing. "She was a *very hard job*. Wouldn't hold a pose. Kept breaking into my concentration. Talk, talk, talk. We have nothing in common."

"Nothing in common?" I repeated the words slowly, I liked them so much. "You mean not like you and me."

Donald reached into his pocket for the sheet of red stickers. He peeled one off. "I mean not like you and me," he said.

I closed my eyes and saw sparklers and shooting stars and red stickers that said SOLD.

When I opened them, I saw the CitiArt gallery walls hung with works in oils and watercolors and tempera. I saw portraits that were full face, three quarter, and profile. I saw studies of hands and feet that looked like hands and feet. I saw that at CitiArt I would *not* be the best artist in the school. I saw that even though art was something I never took seriously, it was what I wanted to do more than anything. I saw that at CitiArt I had a lot to learn that Hilyard could not teach.

"Is there anything you want to know about this?" Donald asked, taking my hand.

"Yes," I said, nodding. "How do people get accepted here?"

"They take the test and submit a portfolio of their work."

So I knew exactly what I needed to do next.

·8·

When I got home, I took down my show and labeled every picture that had been sold.

Then I put them into a folder. Here was my portfolio.

The CitiArt test was not filling in bubbles with a number-two pencil. It was drawing a still life, a portrait, and an abstract design with a number-three pencil.

After the test, Mrs. Wong treated me and Hermione to hot chocolate.

Hermione told us about her music test. "I had to play three pieces and sight-read one. It was thrilling. Oh, how I hope I get in."

That made two of us.

Paxton? Hilyard? CitiArt? CitiTech? It would be a few months till we knew our future schools. In the meantime, the only thing for sure was that we *had* grown and changed.

The day we heard from the schools, we decided to go to Vinnie's for a slice and a celebration.

Hermione and I both got into CitiArt. Debbie was on the waiting list at Hilyard but had decided to go to CitiTech. Keisha and Christy were headed for Paxton.

Linda Dildine began to cry.

"Why are you crying now?" Debbie snapped.

"Because I'm the only one in our class who got into Hilyard, and you are probably all jealous and angry with me."

"Why should we be jealous and angry with you?" I could hardly look at her, I was so jealous and angry.

"Because . . . because I'm the only one in our whole class who'll get to be a Hilly." She started to sniffle, but I saw a little smile on her lips.

"That's true," I agreed, and then I began to laugh. My soda went down the

wrong pipe, and I couldn't catch my
breath.

"What's so funny?" Linda pounded on
my back.

"How could I be jealous and angry with
you for getting to be a Hilly," I gasped,
"when I'm going to get to be something
so much better?"

"What's that?" Debbie and Keisha and
Christy and Hermione leaned over the
table to hear.

"A *Rosy*," I said.
"I get to be a Rosy."

Hermione clapped her hands in delight.

"And I'm going to be a Hermione."

"I'll be a Keisha." Keisha lifted her paper cup of soda.

We all touched our cups together. "Here's to who we are," Debbie said.

"And to the schools that wanted us," I added, "for who we are."

Graduation morning, our class gathered outside the swing doors to the auditorium, waiting for Mrs. Lee to start playing the graduation march. We hugged and kissed, and for once Linda wasn't the only one crying.

"Form two straight lines the way you did in rehearsal," Mrs. Bober called out as the music began.

Hermione grabbed my arm. "Oh, Rosy," she gasped, suddenly wretched. "It's all over."

I looked through the glass window in the door. I could see my parents and Anitra and Pippa and the Wongs and the Dildines. I saw Donald sitting with Christy's parents and her sister, Dawn. On the

stage were our principal, Dr. Gormley, and our teacher, Mrs. Oliphant. I thought of next year at CitiArt, learning to paint in oils and watercolors with classmates who were really interested in art. I thought of how I had knocked my brains out to get accepted to Hilyard, and wasn't, and how I had been myself to get accepted to CitiArt . . . and was.

I thought about growing and changing.

"It's not all over," I told Hermione, giving her a push through the door. "It's beginning."

Two by two, in our white dresses, we started down the aisle.